THE
TAKing
OF
ROOM
114

Books by Mel Glenn

Poetry

Novels

THE
TAKing
OF
ROOM
114

A Hostage Drama in Poems

MEL GLENN

Lodestar Books
Dutton   New York

No character in this book is intended to represent any actual person;
all the incidents of the story are entirely fictional in nature.

Library of Congress Cataloging-in-Publication Data
Glenn, Mel.
    The taking of Room 114: a hostage drama in poems/Mel Glenn.
        p.   cm.
    Summary: A series of poems reflect the thoughts of school officials,
parents, police, and especially a class of seniors who have been taken
hostage by their high school history teacher.
    ISBN 0-525-67548-5 (alk. paper)
    1. High school students—Poetry.   2. Young adult poetry, American.
[1. High schools—Poetry.   2. Schools—Poetry.   3. Teachers—Poetry.
4. Hostages—Poetry.   5. American poetry.]
PS3557.L447T34   1997
811'.54—dc21   96-45545   CIP   AC

Published in the United States by Lodestar Books,
an affiliate of Dutton Children's Books,
a division of Penguin Books USA Inc.,
375 Hudson Street, New York, New York 10014

Published simultaneously in Canada
by McClelland & Stewart, Toronto

Editor: Rosemary Brosnan   Designer: Barbara Powderly
Printed in the U.S.A.   First Edition   10 9 8 7 6 5

for my son Andrew,
with love

Mr. Wiedermeyer's Senior History Class
Class: H7-02
Room: 114

Class Roster

Douglas Atherton	Eddie Kellerman
Derek Bain	Lynette Kincaid
Patti Bennett	Holly Lester
Omar Clarkson	Brad McCall
Andrew Curran	Morton Potter
Cory Deshayes	Renata Reznitskaya
Devonne Elliot	Justin Singleberry
Rhonda Ellis	Denise Slattery
Kathleen Gennaro	Esther Torres
Alissa Hayley	Franklin Waters
Dwight Henderson	Wing Li Wu

School Personnel, Students, Neighborhood Residents,
Press, and Police

Harry Balinger, police captain
Sherwood Cowley, principal
Vinnie Delvecchio, parent
Roger Dunlop, assistant principal
Shawn Ferguson, student
Traci Finch, spectator
Thomas Findlay, spectator
Cosmo Gennaro, parent
Barbara Gilchrist, teacher
Cherise Graham, TV anchor
Gloria Messinger, teacher's aide
Frank Picardi, emergency unit
Jessica Ruíz, student
David Rush, TV reporter
James Sánchez, police officer
Erik Semler, student
Kevin Slattery, brother of Denise
Aaron Washington Jr., teacher
Joseph Wiedermeyer, teacher
Bruno Willis, spectator
Sandi Wilmat, parent

Farewell, thou child of my right hand, and joy;
My sin was too much hope of thee, loved boy. . . .
Rest in soft peace. . . .

Ben Jonson
"On My First Son"

THE COURTYARD

June 16th

8:00 A.M.

Before Class

Lynette Kincaid
Patti Bennett

Can you believe this?
> Like everything else 'round here, slow.

You call this breakfast?
> Better than what you'd get inside.

Patti, this bagel's a rock.
> I bought it, I didn't bake it.

How long do we have to wait out here?
> 'Til they give out *The Talisman.*

What's a talisman, anyway?
> You know, the yearbook, duh.

I know *that,* but what is it?
> Beats me.

I'm thinkin' of splitting, wanna come?
> But Wiedermeyer's giving a test.

Like I care? The term's over.
> He can still flunk us.

Who keeps a senior back?
> I don't know.

Well, Wiedermeyer won't, he's too nice.
> Yeah, he's pretty cool for an old guy.

How long we gotta wait?

Derek Bain
Rhonda Ellis

We gotta wait out here?
> That's what I hear.

Why can't they just distribute them in homeroom?
> That would be too easy.

Man, I can't wait to see it.
> Why?

Like it sums up high school, I don't know.
> Who wants to remember high school?

I do, man—the parties, the girls, the fun.
> That's not high school, that's *after* high school.

I still want the yearbook—so my friends can sign it.
> Me? I want it so the world can see
> What I looked like *before* I became a star.

Hey, Madonna, I think the line's never goin' to move.
> Derek, you wouldn't happen to have
> An extra term paper on you, would you?

You're kiddin' me.
> No, I need it for Wiedermeyer's class.

Just tell him stars don't do no term papers.
> Think he'll go for that?

Omar Clarkson

Man, I'm wiped.
What time is it?
Eight o'clock?
In the morning?
Feels like I just got offa work.
For six dollars an hour my boss thinks he owns me:
Mop this,
Stock that,
Count this,
Move that.
What a pain in the ass.
Can't believe I'm actually standing—sort of—
On this stupid line for a stupid yearbook.
I'm gonna have all my friends sign it.
All my teachers, too:
Gilchrist, Washington, Klein, Parker,
Even old man Wiedermeyer.
You know, he's a lot like my boss—crazy.
Hey, Esther, this line moving or what?
Girl, you look so fine this morning.
You know you want me.

Esther Torres

Omar, you stop playin',
You hear me?
Stop foolin' around, I'm serious.
Get your hands offa me,
Or you're gonna lose somethin' vital.
Hey, octopus-man, I told you,
Leave me a-lone!
What?
What did you call me?
Hey, just because
I don't find you the man of my dreams
Don't mean I'm a lesbian,
And even if I was, what's it to you?
You guys are all pigs.
What am I lookin' for?
Well, it sure ain't you, babe.
Let's just say it's somethin' more . . . spiritual
And leave it at that, OK?
Yeah, yeah. I can see the line's not movin'.

Kathleen Gennaro

When the nuns caught me smoking,
They rapped my knuckles with a ruler
And told my mother; she didn't believe them.
I was eleven.
When my mother caught me smoking,
She flushed the pack down the toilet
And told my father; he grounded me.
I was twelve.
What's everyone getting in an uproar for?
I don't do coke.
I don't do crack.
I don't do heroin.
I'm a good girl.
Hey, if I want to smoke,
It's my business, right?
I'm seventeen and no one can tell me what to—
That's him, that's him!
That's the guy from my history class,
The one I want to know better.
Hold my place in line, will you?
I'm going to ask him if he's got a cigarette.

Cory Deshayes

Yearbook line?
Get stuffed.
You won't find me waitin' for that crap.
Bad enough I've spent six months at this school,
I gotta remember it, too?
This is my fourth school.
My family moves around a lot.
You got a problem with that?
I did just enough to pass —
Even Wiedermeyer's class,
Though the old guy threatened to flunk me,
For a stupid thing like homework.
But the real action is outside of school.
There's only one reason for high school that I can see:
Girls — and more girls.
Think I'll take a walk 'round the block
And grab a smoke.
You never know who you might meet.
But I'll be back for Wiedermeyer's class.
There's a girl in that class I want to know better.
Her name is Kathleen.

Wing Li Wu

I do not have time to get my yearbook now.
I come early to school today to meet my friend, Tuyet.
But I must be truthful.
I am also embarrassed for my English.
It is not good enough to write in people's yearbooks.
So, please excuse me.
I must find my friend.

Dwight Henderson

Hey, Wu,
Where you goin'?
Ain't you gonna wait for your yearbook?
I can't wait to see mine, especially the football pages.
I'm gonna have all my teammates sign it,
Even if I skip a few classes today.
I may not have played a lotta minutes,
But who's gonna know that years from now,
When they look at the team picture
And see me standin' right next to the star quarterback?

Andrew Curran

Only a few more days
And I can get on
With the rest of my life.
I'm going to a good college
And plan to major in biology.
I want to make a scientific contribution to the world.
People will point to my picture in the yearbook and say,
"There's Andrew Curran, I knew him when . . ."

Morton Potter

Only a few more days
And I can get on
With the rest of my life.
I'm going to a decent college
And plan to major in hotel management.
I want to make a culinary contribution to the world.
People will point to my picture in the yearbook and say,
"There's Morton Potter, I knew him when . . ."

Holly Lester

Only a few more days
And I can get on
With the rest of my life.
I'm not going to college
And plan to go out on the road.
I want to make a musical contribution to the world.
People will point to my picture in the yearbook and say,
"There's Holly Lester, I knew her when . . ."

Denise Slattery

Hey, watch where you're goin', pal.
Can't you see I'm pregnant?
"Who could miss it?"
That's cute, funnyman.
I should punch you out
For sayin' stuff like that.
I'd do it, too,
But I wouldn't want to mess up my baby.
As soon as I can,
I'm gonna grab my yearbook
And then my diploma
And head on down South
And let my grammy take care of me
While I take care of my Precious.
(You like that name?)
My mother?
I hope she rots,
Never you mind why.

Why, Douglas, that's very kind of you,
Bringin' me that chair.
You may be a nerd,
But you sure are a gentleman, too, 'preciate it.
Believe me, the baby's father could learn somethin' from you.

Douglas Atherton

My father drives a cab.
My mother works in a doctor's office.
They have never gone on a vacation.
They have always saved every extra penny.
In so many words they have told me,
"You, darling, are the light of our lives,
The main reason for our existence.
You'll go to college, and then law school,
And then who knows what will happen?"
They have mortgaged their future for mine.
So how do I tell them,
At the brink of my graduation,
Standing in line for my yearbook,
The pressure of their sacrifice,
The size of the sum they will spend
To put me through school,
Is too much for me to bear?

Alissa Hayley

My father runs a shoe store.
My mother sells cosmetics.
They have always taken vacations together.
They have always spent their money freely.
In so many words they have told me,
"You, sweetheart, are now eighteen years old
And perfectly capable of living on your own.
You'll find a job and move out.
And then who knows what will happen?"
They have mortgaged my future for theirs.
So how do I tell them,
At the brink of my graduation,
Standing in line for my yearbook,
The emotional neglect I feel,
The size of the debt I'll incur
To put myself through school,
Is too much for me to bear?

Brad McCall

Hey,
There goes Mr. Wiedermeyer.
    "Hey, Mr. W., what's up?"
Man, some teachers look so old,
They look like they live in Jurassic Park.
Man, some teachers have been here so long,
They look like they've taught Fred Flintstone.
Man, some teachers don't teach history,
They look like they remember it.
    "Just waiting for my yearbook."
Man, some teachers look so anemic,
They look like they run on chalk dust.
Man, some teachers act so weird,
They look like they never had a normal life.
Man, but some teachers are nice, after all,
They look like they really want to help you.
    "Hey, Mr. W., you're looking fantastic today.
    Wanna shoot a few hoops with me later?"

Renata Reznitskaya

In Russia,
There were lines for
Toothpaste,
Toilet paper, and
Fruit in the market.
Basic necessities.
In America,
There are lines for
Amusement park rides,
Free, how-you-say, giveaways, and
High school yearbooks.
Nonbasic frivolities.
Perhaps I will come back tomorrow
And receive my yearbook then,
When the line is not so long.
Instead, I will use this early time now
To go to my teachers, personally,
And thank them for all they've taught me,
Especially Mr. Wiedermeyer.
I do not think there will be
A long line of students for that.

Justin Singleberry

Hey, let's get this line moving already.
I can't hang around here all day.
I got places to go, stuff to do,
And you guys are holding me up.
Can't you mail me my yearbook—
Care of American Express, Paris?
That's right, Paris.
I'm packing my book bag
With underwear and art supplies,
And as soon as I get my ticket,
I'm going to see all the great cities of Europe
While there is time,
And draw the local people as they go
Back and forth between work and home.
So when you see my picture in the yearbook,
Standing still in cap and gown,
It will probably be the last time
You see me standing still.
Au revoir, mes amis.
I'll send you all postcards,
But right now I gotta get out of here.

Devonne Elliot
Eddie Kellerman

He's the best history teacher I ever had.
>Well, he's the worst I ever had. What did he give you?
Ninety-five. You?
>Seventy-five.
There you go, judging just by the grade.
>What else should I judge by?
What you learned, what he showed you about the world.
>He showed me a seventy-five.
I still say Wiedermeyer's the best.
>You don't know what you're talkin' about.
Hey, here come the yearbooks.

THE CALL

June 16th

9:00 A.M.

Classes in Session

Roger Dunlop, assistant principal

Listen, young man, what's your name?
Well, Eddie Kellerman,
You can't park yourself in the middle of the hallways.
You're blocking traffic and causing major congestion.
People have to detour around you.
I must keep these lanes clear, you understand.
I know you want to get your book autographed,
But what if I let everyone cut class
To get their yearbook signed?
Kids would be backed up for miles.
What would that be like?
"Fun"?
You can't have fun here; this is school.
Hurry up now, get back to class.
What is it, Ms. Messinger?
You should know better than to run in the halls.
Did I see what note?
From whom?
What do you mean he won't open the door?

Ms. Gloria Messinger, teacher's aide

I tried to collect his attendance.
Mr. Wiedermeyer never keeps his door locked.
Then I looked down and found this note.
Here, you read it for yourself.
I think he's gone off the deep end.

Teacher's Note #1

It starts slowly:
A cough here, a cackle there,
A dropped book, a pushed chair.
Of themselves, separate moments in an ordered universe,
But in progression, measured beats to a crescendo of chaos.
>He hit me,
>He took my pen,
>She pushed me,
>She dissed me.

Or,
>I have to go to the bathroom,
>I need to see the nurse,
>I gotta find my counselor,
>I must talk to the coach.

Or,
>Can I make up the homework?
>Can I make up the test?
>Can I make up the term?
>Can I make up last term?

Yes, my children,
You all did it,
Including you, Michael.
You all did it.
Don't worry, it's so quiet now, you can hear an eraser drop.
They're giving me their undivided attention.
I couldn't possibly let them go.

Roger Dunlop, assistant principal

Mr. Wiedermeyer,	No Answer
I'm knocking	No Answer
On the door.	No Answer
Would you mind	No Answer
Opening it up, please?	No Answer
Are you OK?	No Answer
Is the class OK?	No Answer
Is any unauthorized person with you?	No Answer
Any unauthorized student?	No Answer
Any unauthorized adult?	No Answer
Please open the door.	No Answer
You leave me	No Answer
No choice.	No Answer
Ms. Messinger,	No Answer
Call 911.	No Answer
I'm knocking	No Answer
On the door,	No Answer
Mr. Wiedermeyer.	No Answer
Who's Michael?	No Answer

Sherwood Cowley, principal
(Public Address Announcement)

Mr. Wiedermeyer,
This is Principal Cowley on the loudspeaker.
Can you hear me?
Please report to the main office.
We need to have your records now.
It is a matter of great urgency.
Mr. Wiedermeyer,
Please listen to this announcement.
I don't know how long
We can let this situation continue.
Mr. Wiedermeyer,
Can you hear me?
Am I getting through to you,
Loud and clear?

Mr. Dunlop, you called the police, didn't you?

Unit 4

Yeah, we got it, on our way.
Possible disturbance at the high school.
Hope no one killed a teacher.
Remember that from a few years ago?
Yeah, Tower High, they didn't say.
You know I went to that school.
It's a miracle how kids get outta there.

Cherise Graham,
channel 5, local news anchor

WE INTERRUPT OUR REGULAR BROADCAST TO
BRING YOU THIS LATE-BREAKING STORY. POLICE
HAVE BEEN CALLED TO TOWER HIGH SCHOOL TO
INVESTIGATE A POSSIBLE HOSTAGE SITUATION.
ACCORDING TO OUR SOURCES, A SENIOR
HISTORY CLASS HAS BEEN TAKEN OVER BY A
PERSON OR PERSONS UNKNOWN. THERE ARE
NO REPORTS OF ANY INJURIES. THERE ARE NO
REPORTS OF ANY BOMBS. POLICE AND
EMERGENCY PERSONNEL ARE IN THE PROCESS
OF EVACUATING THE BUILDING. OUR MOBILE
UNIT IS ON THE WAY, TOO, AND AS SOON AS WE
CAN, WE WILL BE BRINGING YOU A LIVE UPDATE.
AND NOW BACK TO OUR REGULAR PROGRAM.

Sherwood Cowley, principal

Thank you for coming so quickly, gentlemen.
Detectives Balinger and Picardi, is it?
I don't believe it, Mr. Wiedermeyer, of all people.
That man has been here for more than twenty years.
Of course I know him.
Said hi to him just the other day.
Yes, he is hardly ever absent,
Though last year about this time,
He was out for a week, maybe two,
For some personal business, I think.
Yes, he often keeps to himself.
Yes, he is always up-to-date with his paperwork.
No, I don't know if he's angry about anything.
No, I don't know if he has a mental history.
No, I don't know if he has any political affiliations.
He was married, divorced a long time ago.
Is he strange?
Is he odd?
I really couldn't tell you.
Yes, more than twenty years, a lifetime of teaching.
Had anything been wrong,
Don't you think we would have known?

      Yes, Ms. Messinger, what is it?
      Another note?

Teacher's Note #2

You have been unruly,
And the usual punishments
That are meted out for violations
No longer work.
Zeroes,
Phone calls home,
Detention, suspensions,
Can't shake you out of your
Comas of indifference.
I've seen it all:
Freshman Fog,
Sophomore Slump,
Junior Jokes,
Senior Slide.
What do you care about?
What's on your minds?
I think I'll keep you a while longer,
You, too, Michael.
Just to find out.

Harry Balinger, police captain
Frank Picardi, emergency unit

Everyone out of the building?
    All clear, Captain.
What do we know?
    Not a whole lot.
Is there a phone in the classroom?
    It's been disconnected.
No way of establishing contact, then?
    Not unless we're ready to bust down the door.
The notes are in his handwriting?
    Confirmed, though he might be forced to write them.
You mean someone else is in there?
    Could be, we haven't heard anything.
Might be one of his students, a grudge.
    Or maybe an ex-student.
Assuming it's just him, what do you suppose set him off?
    I couldn't even guess.
We know anything about his politics?
    Nope, not yet, got some people on it.
Have we contacted his ex-wife?
    Secretary says they can't locate her.
I want you to check out a student's name — Michael.
    No last name?
No.

Harry Balinger, police captain

You read the headlines
That are forgotten the next day:
    "Student Goes Berserk in Dorm"
    "Teen Kills Teen for Bicycle"
    "Businessman Jumps from Bridge"
    "Mother's Boyfriend Drowns Tot"
Private tortures
Ending in public spectacle.
Serpentine demons
Strangling common sense.
Mr. Wiedermeyer,
What set you off?
What memories were triggered,
What words were said
That pushed you over the edge?
Most of us toe the line of sanity,
But how many cross it to madness?
Mr. Wiedermeyer,
Is it too late for you to step back
To our side of the line, I wonder,
And put to rest
The evil and craziness within us all?

Sandy Wilmat, parent

Where is my child?
Is he alive, is he dead?
Tell me, I got a right to know.
Oh, my God, he's dead, then.
Don't tell me to calm down.
I heard it on TV,
Some madman with a gun,
Maybe even a bomb?
Why don't they let us get closer?
What?
He's a junior.
Yes, a junior.
What are you saying?
A senior class?
Are you sure?
Oh, thank you, thank you, God.
The other mothers?
Sure, I feel bad for 'em.
Look, I gotta go,
I gotta go find my son.

Jessica Ruíz, student

They didn't tell us nothin'.
All I know, it's a free day.
I can go to the movies, the park, or the mall.
I can do anything I want,
But maybe I'll just go home and sleep.

Erik Semler, student

They didn't tell us much,
But what do I care?
I'm going down to the park
And shoot some threes.
Everyone says I got no shot for the pros.
I'm gonna show them all.

Shawn Ferguson, student

They hardly told us anything,
But who's arguing?
Gives me a chance to grab some breakfast.
Maybe I'll check out if they're hiring.
I could use some extra cash.
Besides, work's gotta be more interesting than school.

Traci Finch, spectator

Oh, those poor kids,
Locked up with that awful madman.
The police must use extreme caution—
Negotiators, clergy, and the like.
Time is on their side.
Every minute there's a dialogue
Lengthens the possibility
They will all survive.
Every minute we use common sense
Increases the chances for success.
Don't rush into anything, I beg you.
Remember Waco.
I weep for the future of America
If these unfortunate youngsters
Died while everyone just ran around
Shooting.

Thomas Findlay, spectator

Oh, those poor kids,
Locked up with that awful madman.
The police must take direct action—
SWAT teams, concussion grenades, and the like.
Time is on his side.
Every minute there's a dialogue
Lengthens the possibility
They will all die.
Every minute we don't use common sense
Increases the chances for failure.
Do something now, I beg you.
Remember Entebbe.
I weep for the future of America
If these unfortunate youngsters
Died while everyone just sat around
Talking.

Aaron Washington Jr., teacher

The guy's brilliant, simply brilliant.
You don't believe this is a real hostage situation,
Do you?
Hear me out.
The whole thing's a trick, a ruse.
He teaches history, right?
Maybe it's a class project
And they're studying terrorism.
Look, I've known Wiedermeyer for years.
A bit strange, I'll admit,
But he would never do anything to hurt kids.
He has kids or a kid of his own,
I think, I'm not sure.
Everybody should just stay cool.
You'll see—the class will walk out
With huge smiles across their faces.
They will all get A's for acting.
The guy's brilliant, simply brilliant.

Barbara Gilchrist, teacher

The guy's nuts, simply nuts.
I mean, why would anybody want
To take them hostage?
Why would anybody want
To spend more time with them?
Let me tell you, six-and-a-half hours a day
Is more than enough time with these monsters.
When I first started teaching,
I thought I could make a difference.
Now the only difference I see
Is the number of lines in my face.
When I first started teaching,
Wiedermeyer had been here for years.
How should I know what flipped him out?
I punched a blackboard once.
It's that kind of a job.
Maybe he got tired of all the crap, who knows?
The guy's nuts, simply nuts.

David Rush, TV reporter

WE ARE STANDING HERE, A BLOCK AWAY FROM
THE SCHOOL. THE POLICE WILL NOT LET US GET
ANY CLOSER. HERE IS WHAT WE KNOW: ONE OR
MORE GUNMEN ARE HOLDING A SENIOR HISTORY
CLASS HOSTAGE. I AM STANDING WITH SEVERAL
STUDENTS WHO HAVE BEEN EVACUATED. DO
YOU FELLAS HAVE ANY COMMENTS REGARDING
THIS TENSE SITUATION?

    IT'S VERY EXCITING.

    COOL. I HOPE THEY BLOW THE SICK DUDE
        AWAY.

    HEY, MAN, WHEN IS THIS GONNA BE ON TV?

    HI, MOM.

THANK YOU AND NOW BACK TO THE STUDI—NOT
YET? THEN, IF I MAY, A PHILOSOPHICAL POINT:
ONE WONDERS, WHO ARE THESE STUDENTS?
HOW COME THEY WERE CHOSEN, IF YOU WILL,
TO COME TO THIS CLASS, TO SUFFER THIS

ORDEAL? WHAT FORCES CONSIGNED THEM TO THIS FATE? WHO ARE THEY? WHAT ARE THEIR DREAMS? AND WILL THEY SURVIVE TO PURSUE THOSE DREAMS? FOR NOW, WE CAN ONLY WAIT. . . .

THE CLASS

Lynette Kincaid

In middle school I felt so secure,
Surrounded by the friendly people I knew.
The teachers said hello when I passed them in the halls.
My friends and I would talk about them
And about boys.
In high school I felt so insecure.
I stared at the strangers around me.
Nobody said hello.
Right in the middle of the hall I started to cry.
At first, no one noticed.
Then a girl came up and asked if I was OK.
"I can't find my homeroom," I sniffled.
"Don't worry," she said. "I'll take you there.
I know how you feel—scared, huh?"
I'll never forget how kind Patti was.
I knew then high school was gonna be all right.

Lynette Kincaid

Instead of drawing triangles in math class,
I'm drawing hearts with arrows through them.
Instead of calculating the height of line A,
I'm wondering what opening line
I can use to get him to talk to me.
What angle I can figure out so he'll notice me.
Mike sits two rows
And a thousand miles away.
If I say something to him first,
Will he think I'm too pushy?
If I say nothing to him,
Will I wait forever?
Maybe I'll pass him my homework
With triangles, squares, and circles on it,
Not to mention a few X's and O's on the bottom.
Teacher, I can figure out all the problems you give us,
Except how to get from
Point A to Point B with him.

Lynette Kincaid

I know I've been out of school for two months.
At Mike's house. What do you think we did?
Don't be surprised that I've had sex.
Most girls my age have done it.
Mike's eighteen, dropped out of school last term.
I found out that sex may be good for the moment,
But the moment doesn't last.
I thought he loved me,
But all he wanted was sex.
Oh, he promised me the moon and the stars
And the rest of the universe.
Had I known that he wanted so little,
I wouldn't have given him
So much of myself.

Lynette Kincaid

As a senior,
I do homework, occasionally;
Go to class, when I feel like it;
Hang out, constantly.
What can they do to me?
I got enough credits to graduate.
Life's too short to worry about
Term papers and book reports.
I'd rather worry about finding
A parking space for my new car—
A bribe from my father to stay in school.
Look at that freshman geek over there,
Running to beat the bell.
What's the rush?
High school? You can have it.
I'm a senior; I got my wheels.
I got a right to be on cruise control.

Lynette Kincaid

I'll catch up with you in a second, Patti.
What we got, Wiedermeyer?
Bor-ing, man,
Nothing ever happens in his class.
Hell, nothing ever happens in this whole damn school,
Nothing that I can see anyway.
Look, Patti,
You wanna split?
There's gas in the tank,
Beer in the trunk, and
Guys by the park.
Girl, it's time to rock and roll.
When you gonna realize
School's a trap, not a trip?
When you gonna get your freedom?
When you're old enough for social security?
Not me, I'm outta here.
You coming or what?
No?
Later, then.

Patti Bennett

Papa, when I was six,
You came into my room and scared away the monsters.
I still want you to come into my room and
Scare away the doubts I have about starting high school.
You say I'll do all right.
I say I'm scared silly.
You say the teachers will all love me.
I say how will they know who I am?
You say I'm a big girl now.
I say I'm only fourteen years old.
Papa, I'd like you to tell me
Everything's going to be all right,
That I'll make new friends,
That I'll get a high average,
That I will be able to find my own way.
Papa, is this outfit OK?
Oh, you have to say that.

Patti Bennett

My father wanted a son.
Surprise, Papa, you got me.
My father wanted someone
    to play ball with,
    to build a tree house with,
    to go fishing with.
Instead, he got someone who wanted
    to go to the movies,
    to ice-skate in the park,
    to go shopping downtown.
I see the confused look on his face
As I drag him to one more sale.
It's OK, Papa,
I'll wear my game face
When we go to the ballpark next Friday night.
Gotta compromise, right, Papa?
I can learn how to be your son,
Even if I'm a girl.
And you can learn to appreciate me,
Because I'm the person who loves you,
Regardless of gender.

Patti Bennett

Softball scores sound like football scores:
17–14, 20–10, 24–12.
As I wait in the batter's box
The coach goes through a series of signs.
I don't have a clue what he's talking about
And strike out on four pitches.
One pitch was over my head and
I couldn't have reached it with a ladder.
"Good eye," my coach said.
Yeah, right.
I'm playing, or rather standing, in right field
For all the wrong reasons
To satisfy all the wrong people —
My coach, my teammates, and
Most of all, my father.
I'll be glad when the season's over,
So I can strike out on my own.

Patti Bennett

You want me to sign your yearbook?
Sure, I'd love to.
No, I'm not with the others
On the girls' softball page.
Didn't I tell you?
Quit last year after the season.
Too many things to do.
You know, college applications and stuff.
Yeah, I'm going away to school.
I'll be living in a dorm.
Scared? Yeah, kinda, I guess so.
But I'm more excited than scared,
Know what I mean?
I hope I have enough credits.
I'll just die if I don't graduate.
It'll be way cool to start a new life.
Thanks. That *is* a good picture of me.

Patti Bennett

Later then, Lynette.
Don't do anything I wouldn't do.
You probably will, though.
You always have.
You get your license
And your own car
And your father lets you go anywhere.
I get my license
And no car
And my father doesn't let me out of the house.
You have a curfew,
Ignore it, and your father says nothing.
I have a curfew,
Ignore it, and my father grounds me for a month.
You cut class and it's no big deal.
I cut class and the roof falls on my head.
So you go on and have a good time.
I'll think of you,
Especially as I walk into Wiedermeyer's class.

What the—

Derek Bain

I'm not sure if he left,
Or she just threw him out.
I'm not sure if he loved me,
Or just loved the idea of havin' a kid.
I'm not sure if he bought me presents,
Or he just promised them to me.
I am sure I loved him,
Even though that love was hardly returned.
One time he hit my mother.
I bit his leg.
He flung me across the room,
Like some ball.
Only I didn't bounce.
Now I don't have a father.
It don't make no difference if
He left or she just threw him out.
I still miss him.

Derek Bain

My new stepfather's not too bad,
But the daughter he brought with him
Tortures me night and day,
Always in the bathroom,
Always in my business.
Phoebe, what a goofy name,
Like in *Catcher in the Rye*,
Which I just happen to be readin' in English.
I hope she doesn't follow me around
With a packed suitcase, like in the book.
"I love my new family," my mother says.
But I don't know if I do.
I miss the time she and I
Were alone, together.
Our tiny family felt more whole,
More real than the fake politeness
I have to show at dinnertime.
Why'd she have to marry again?
We were doin' all right, just the two of us.

Derek Bain

I wish I had my own car,
But a license comes first.
I wish I had some extra money,
But I really don't want to work for Mickey D's.
What I'd like to do is jump into a Trans Am
And hit the open road.
School's OK, even good on some days.
But it's always the same routine.
I want to travel the two-lane highways of America
And not know where (or with whom)
I'll be sleeping the next night.
I feel restless
And horny
Pretty much all of the time.
There has to be more to life,
But I don't know what the more is.
I think I'll take a shower, a cold one.
Then maybe I'll do a little math homework.

Derek Bain

Hallelujah!
Startin' tomorrow
I'll have my

> Diplomatic passport,
> Carte blanche,
> Season box seat,
> Exit visa,
> Calling card,
> Letter of transit,
> Papal dispensation,
> Lifetime guarantee,
> Safe-conduct pass,
> Ticket to ride.

I passed my road test
On the very first try.
First thing I'm gonna do is
Take my mother out
For a long, long drive.

Derek Bain

Hey, man, I'm chill.
Feelin' no pain, no way.
I think I got enough credits to graduate.
I think I got a job lined up for the summer.
And I think my bratty stepsister is goin' to camp.
Me and my stepdad are gettin' real tight.
He takes me to places like ball games and auto shows.
He gives me money when I need it,
And even when I don't.
But best of all?
My mom's really enjoyin' herself.
For the first time I can remember
She's crackin' jokes and lookin' good.
Hey, man, things couldn't be better.
What's up? History? No sweat.

What's up?
Is this a joke?
I gotta go to the DMV
And pick up my plates.
You crazy, man?
Put that thing down.

Rhonda Ellis

I tape all the soaps,
Watch *Entertainment Tonight*,
Read *Variety*,
And picture myself being interviewed
On the Letterman show.
I watch all the old movies,
Read theater reviews,
Buy all the movie magazines,
And figure after high school
I'm going to be a big star.
"Be a teacher," my mother says.
"Be an accountant," my father says.
Did Meryl Streep's mother
Urge her to develop lesson plans?
Did Julia Roberts' father
Urge her to balance the books?
Even my brother butts in with
"Why can't you be your real self?
You're always actin' stuck-up, phony."
I *am* my real self,
Especially when I'm playing the part of
Someone else.

Rhonda Ellis

"Next."

> I am so nervous about this audition.
>
> I hope I don't blow my lines.
>
> Look at Nicole Tucker over there—so cool.
>
> I hope she dies,
>
> Onstage, that is.

"Next."

> I don't know why they say
>
> "Break a leg" before you go on.
>
> Does that mean you're part of a cast?
>
> Get a grip, Rhonda,
>
> Don't lose it.

"Next."

> I'm next, God help me.
>
> Got to admit Nicole was good.
>
> But I can be better.
>
> Here goes nothing and
>
> Everything.

"Thank you very much. We'll let you know."

58

Rhonda Ellis

Instead of the star,
I'm the understudy, hoping that
Juliet falls out of the balcony,
Nora's house collapses on her,
Emily never finds Grover's Corners
And Lady Macbeth files for divorce.
In the second grade I played a cabbage.
It was a roll-on part.
In the sixth grade I played a tree.
Branching out, you might say.
I've always been the supporting player,
Never the lead.
I've always been the understudy,
Never the star.
I can't tell you how many roles
I've lost to Nicole Tucker,
Just because she's prettier than me.
The spotlight always falls on her
While I spend my life
Waiting in the wings.

Rhonda Ellis

When I told Nicole Tucker
To break a leg,
I didn't think she would
Take me seriously.
But she did.
She fell off her bicycle,
And I fell into her part.
I went to visit her in the hospital
And told her, stretching the truth a bit,
How sorry I was she had injured herself.
"Oh, it's so nice of you to visit me," she said.
I didn't feel so nice, inside.
I felt, in the unspoken competition between us,
I had won by default.
Still and all, the show must go on, right?
Thanks, Nicole, for my big break—
And yours.

60

Rhonda Ellis

"Mr. Wiedermeyer,
I'm sorry I didn't get the
Term paper in on time.
I know it's due today,
But I fell victim to a disease going around,
Senioritis!
To tell you the truth,
I don't much care what happens in the
First, Second, or Third World.
I got troubles of my own."
     That's what I would *like* to tell him.
     Think he'd go for it?
     Nah, better to give him this note from my mother
     Telling how I had rehearsal all week.
     At least it's the truth.

Mr. Wiedermeyer,
Sorry I didn't get the—
What is this, a class skit?
No one told me.
What is my role?

Omar Clarkson

Things my brother says to me
About life in general:
    "Get outta my room."
    "You're a butthead."
    "Your turn to do the laundry."
    "Take a shower for a change."
And high school in particular:
    "Can't believe they let you in high school."
    "Don't talk to me in the halls."
    "You're too young to look at girls like that."
    "On the football team with me? Get serious."
I still love you, jerk.
Happy Birthday, Stephon.

Omar Clarkson

Things teachers say to me all the time:
    "Why are you late?"
    "Take out paper for a pop quiz."
    "You get a zero."
    "Where's your homework?"
    "Open your book to page . . ."
    "Where's your textbook?"
    "The homework for tomorrow is . . ."
    "There will be a test on Friday."
    "May I have your attention, please?"
I swear,
Teachers must get together
To rehearse these things.
It's about time they got some new lines
To play back as their recorded messages.

Omar Clarkson

Things I'd like to hear from girls:
"You're so cool, Omar."
"You're really hot."
"I love your body."
"Of course I'll dump my boyfriend for you."
"Nobody's at my house tonight, come over."
"You're the nicest guy I ever met."
"You're the wildest guy I ever met."
"You're so strong."
"Hold me."
"I'll love you forever."
In the daytime,
Girls rush from one classroom to another,
Hardly saying more than, "Hi, Omar."
But at night,
They slowly parade before my eyes
In the great erotic stage show of my dreams.

Omar Clarkson

Things I should tell myself (but don't):
    "I'm not so bad looking."
    "Start my term paper."
    "What's the worst she could say, no?"
    "Stop watching *Beavis and Butthead*, kid stuff."
    "Stay away from junk food."
    "Talk to my father once in a while."
    "Write my brother, Stephon, a letter."
    "Study for my math midterm."
    "Save some money from my measly paycheck."
The world is full of possibilities,
If I can just hit that alarm-clock button
And not fall back asleep.
Five more minutes, please.

Omar Clarkson

Waiting in line
To go up the steps of the stage
To receive my diploma,
I can imagine my parents just out of earshot.
My mother will tell me to stand up straight.
My father will tell me I did all right—
Not great, just all right.
By then, I will know how to listen to my own voice
And not go through life
Listening to others who think
They have all the answers for me.
The music will start;
The line will move toward the stairs.
I hope I won't trip up.
I don't think I will.
Now?
I got history.
Where'd I put my homework?

Hey, Mr. Wiedermeyer,
I made it just at the bell.
Hey, what's this?
Quit waving that thing around.
All right, all right, I'm moving,
I hear what you're saying to me.

Esther Torres

My mother sleeps around,
And with each new friend she collects
I have the hope
That both of them will be happy.
The honeymoon lasts for a short while
Until her friend tries to become my friend—
Know what I'm sayin'?
Fingers lightly dance on my knee or shoulder
Until they try to travel upward or downward.
I sit there, frozen,
My eyes turned toward the wall.
I never tell my mother anything
Because she would say it's my own fault.
When the last one put his hand on my breast,
I screamed, stood up, and kicked him between the legs.
My mother couldn't understand
Why he left so quickly.
What I want is a boyfriend of my own,
One I don't have to share.

Esther Torres

When my French teacher asked me
For the first five homeworks,
I couldn't answer her.
When my math teacher asked me
Why I had failed the midterm,
I couldn't answer him.
When my guidance counselor asked me
Why I had failed three subjects,
I couldn't answer her.
How could I tell them all that
I, in my shame, had no answers for anyone,
Least of all myself.
Oh, dear God, I feel so lost.
One thing I'm sure of, though,
Everything's my own damn fault.

Esther Torres

Sunday,
when
I
went
to
Sunday, when I went to Church, I knelt and crossed myself.
I
looked
at
the
altar
and
prayed
for
God's
forgiveness.

Esther Torres

I found a man, a real man,
One who will lead me out of the darkness
Into the light of beauty and happiness.
Though I share him with others,
I do not mind.
Though I worship him from afar,
He is deep within my soul and skin.
The passion he arouses in me
Lifts me off my feet.
The softness of his words
Allows me to slumber in peace.
He will never forsake me,
Nor I, him.
He makes my heart cry out in joy.
I have found a man, a real man,
And Jesus is his name.

Esther Torres

I wonder what death is like
And so when our creative writing teacher
Told us to use our imaginations, I did
And described a divine world of
Chariots and cherubim,
Angels with tender mercies
And heavenly choirs calling to me.
When my teacher read my piece,
She thought I wanted to board the celestial railroad
Right away.
She took me to the guidance counselor,
Where I assured both ladies that, even though
My eyes may look toward Elysium,
My feet are firmly planted on the ground.
I may, one day, want to ride that railroad,
But for now I'll reserve my seat
For many years down the line.
I think heaven can wait for me.

Dear God,
If you wish to call me now,
I promise I'll be ready.

Teacher's Note #3
(Transcript of a recent homeroom conversation)

Hey, man, history/homeroom teacher, whatever you are,
You got my freakin' school bus pass?
You know I'm entitled to it.
You know I'm supposed to get it
So I can take this freakin' bus
To go to this freakin' school
And get my freakin' education.
What you mean, you don't have it?
My name's on the list;
I'm supposed to get it, understand?
I'm not interested in no reasons.
I told you, I want that freakin' pass.
So go call my mother,
See if I care.
The only thing she's gonna tell you is
How come he didn't get his freakin' bus pass?
So where is it?

Kathleen Gennaro

Out of that school with white shirts and pleated skirts.
Out of that school with required mass and rigid rules.
I put my foot down last year
And told my parents in no uncertain terms
There was no way in hell
I was going to Catholic high school.
They said that's exactly where I'd be going—
To hell, that is.
My parents, after the Big Fight,
Gave in and prayed for my soul.
I'll worry about my soul later.
I'm having too good a time now.
No uniform rules.
No uniform dress code.
No uniform uniforms.
I love the new books I'm reading.
I love the new work I'm doing.
And the boy next to me in math
Said I was cute.

Kathleen Gennaro

He's in my class again,
And this time I'm gonna talk to him—
If I can get up the nerve.
What if he thinks I'm stupid?
What if I go up to him and say,
"Hey, you're cute, too. Let's go out."
Maybe he'll turn around and say,
"Who are you?"
I'd just die.
Like the song says,
Catholic girls start much too late.
But I'm gonna make up for lost time.
You haven't got a chance, Mark.

Kathleen Gennaro

I want to take romantic walks by the park.
He wants to go bowling.
I'd like to go ballroom dancing.
He'd rather rent a video.
The spark of our first few months together
Has been reduced to a pilot light.
Don't get me wrong, though.
Mark is reliable, trustworthy, and kind,
A Boy Scout without the uniform.
There are dozens of girls in school
Who would be thrilled to have him
If I were stupid enough to let him go.
I'm not stupid.
But even though I settle for that pleasant pilot light,
I do sometimes miss the roaring flames of passion.

Kathleen Gennaro

My grandmother said,
"There's plenty of pasta in the soup."
But all her words of comfort
And predictions of new loves in my future
Did not ease the pain of
Mark breaking up with me.
Our comfortable relationship
Was too comfortable, according to him.
He had found someone else, according to his friends.
"How could you do this to me?" I screamed at him.
"I was gonna tell you," he said sheepishly.
"When?" I said. "Right after the prom?
I never want to see your face again."
I don't need him or any man to make me happy.
This is what I tell myself.
But it still hurts.
Grandma, what can you tell me now?

Kathleen Gennaro

Mark who?
A memory, man.
I can't believe I fell for him.
When he smiled, the whole world felt sunny.
When he held my hand, we were one person.
When he kissed me, we were one soul.
I can't believe he controlled my life.
Guys are scum;
They think with the wrong organ.
All they want to do is
Take you to bed,
Or hang out with their friends,
Or tell you how great they are,
Or order you around as if they own you.
Mark, what a mistake.
I'm swearing off guys for good.
But you gotta know,
This guy in my history class?
His name is Cory.
Man, is he hot.
I see him next period.

You can't tell me what to do.
You can't push me around.
I'm gonna sit where I want.
Cory, is there room next to you?

Cory Deshayes

"Hi."
"How's it goin'?"
"Hey, man, what's up?"
"Later."
People in the halls float by
Like so many schools of fish.
It's a matter of knowing which currents to ride.
There may be official teams,
Like baseball, basketball, and football,
But the unofficial teams of
Geeks, jocks, and cool ones
Are far more important.
You don't want to swim in the wrong circles, man.
You'd go belly-up pretty quickly.
To be with the in crowd
You gotta know how to
Navigate the waters of popularity.
I can be happy here; I know it.
I can do happy, I can do popular,
As long as I know how to swim
Within the right school.

Cory Deshayes

Last week at a friend's party
I lost my virginity—
I think.
I was kind of out of it.
There was a lot of drinkin' goin' on,
With me doin' a lot of it.
The last thing I remember
Is this girl, Melissa, takin' my hand
And leadin' me to the bedroom.
I swear I don't remember what happened after that.
The next thing I do remember
Is Melissa takin' my hand
And leadin' me back to the living room
And sayin' stuff like
How good I was,
How it was special for her,
And could we do it again, real soon.
I said, "Sure, why not?"
Hopin' that next time
I'd remember what my friends say
Is somethin' you never forget.

Cory Deshayes

At the pool hall all the girls
Are in my pocket.
At the basketball game
I can score at will.
At the bowling alley
I can knock them all down,
And at the baseball game
I get to first base,
Steal second,
Take third,
Pump for home,
A grand slam.
It's a great sport, man.
I am the champion of the world,
Super stud, super smooth.
There hasn't been a girl made
That I can't make.
I give them all what they want
And what they want is me.
Relationships?
Nah, I don't have time for such crap.

Cory Deshayes

Hey, Michelle,
What are you talkin' about?
I wasn't hittin' on her.
I wasn't even talkin' to her.
If you wanna know the truth,
She was comin' on to me.
Of course I know she's your best friend.
What does that have to do with anything?
Look, Michelle,
You gotta give me some room here.
Get off my case, will ya?
If you can't trust me by now,
We got nothin' goin',
You hear what I'm sayin'?
Look, Michelle,
Which way is it gonna be?
Hey, what are you cryin' for?
It's really botherin' me.
Look, Michelle,
I gotta split now.
Talk to you later,
OK?
What do you mean, don't bother?

Cory Deshayes

Michelle who?
A memory, man.
I can't believe I fell for her.
When she smiled, the whole world felt sunny.
When she held my hand, we were one person.
When she kissed me, we were one soul.
I can't believe she controlled my life.
Girls are trash;
They can't think at all.
All they want to do is
Refuse you in bed,
Or hang out with their friends,
Or tell you how awful they look,
Or order you around as if they own you.
Michelle, what a mistake.
I'm swearing off girls for good,
But you gotta know,
This girl in my history class?
Her name is Kathleen.
Man, is she hot.
I see her next period.

You can't tell me what to do.
You can't push me around.
I'm gonna sit where I want.
Kathleen, is there room next to you?

Wing Li Wu
(In translation)

When I was twelve,
None of us knew
The color of the sea or sky as we crossed
The South China Sea for Malaysia,
The first step of our journey to America.
We paid much money and had to pay it back with interest
When we got good jobs in the States.
None of us knew
How many days or weeks it would take
Not to feel so cold or wet or hungry.
When the captain said to come on deck,
He pointed to the beach through heavy seas
And said, "We are almost there."
The most horrible thing happened:
The engine died; the boat took on water;
And soon all I heard were screams
As I tried to grab something floating.
I lost my mother and my six-year-old sister.
None of us knew
Why we were allowed to see pictures of freedom
Only to have them cruelly snatched from us.
I still think about this two years later.
I will think about it all my life.

Wing Li Wu

I can hear the rain
And listen to the wind.
I can feel the sun
And understand the moon.
One does not need words
To understand the music of the universe.
I do not know the American idiom yet,
The jokes, the easy laughter in the halls.
My English words feel like ill-fitting clothes.
In school I find a new way
To say what is inside me.
I begin to play the flute,
The notes dancing off this most graceful instrument.
Until my vocabulary in English gets better,
I will practice hard,
Listen to my teacher,
And wait for the day
I can introduce my music in English
With my new language
And play an American tune without mistake.

Wing Li Wu

In America,
It is not enough to make music.
One has to make money, too.
I do not wish for many riches,
Just some new clothes, perhaps.
And, if I am fortunate,
A flute of my own.
I hope I do not ask for too much.
My friend, Tuyet, from the orchestra
Asks me to go to the movies with her.
I tell her I can't.
She is offended and turns away from me.
I have not the money to go
And am too ashamed to tell her.
My music has grown.
My orchestra teacher is pleased with me, I know.
But it is not enough.
I desire friends to share the music of life.
I do not wish to play solo any longer.

Wing Li Wu

There is a tinkle of small chimes
When the customer enters
The little shop I work in after school.
She smiles at the sweet sound
As I walk toward her to make my greeting.
The customer nods pleasantly and goes without noise
To shelves filled with colorful vases.
She then looks at delicate pen-and-ink drawings
Of rice paddies and old women in small villages.
"Very pretty," she says, politely, again smiling.
"Thank you," I reply.
"I will be back later," she says
To ease her exit without purchase.
The store is quiet once more.
I do my history homework now.
The old women look at me.
I hear the chimes again
And think for a moment
It's Mother who has come back to see me,
Her eyes filled with tears of pride at my success.

Wing Li Wu

I have American friends;
I speak American words;
I learn American history;
I make American money.
But all the while
My soul hungers for its true home
Back across the sea,
Back across the years.
Pining for the past
Points me in the wrong direction.
I must improve my grades
So I can get into a good college
And start my life.
Physics is very hard for me.
I fall asleep over vector problems
While my aunt pours more tea into me
To keep my eyes from closing.
I have a big test today
Right after my next class,
History.

I don't understand what Mr. Wiedermeyer is doing.
Why is he acting so strangely?

Teacher's Note #4

Here's my next note
For you to read.
Here's my next note
For you to heed.
Tower High School students:
You can't read,
You can't write,
You can't speak,
You can't fight.
You sleep all day,
A cap on your head,
Never pay attention,
To whatever is said.
You can't think,
You do not know,
You won't reflect,
You're much too slow.
Where's your education
Heading these days?
Nowhere, but through
A Byzantine maze.

88

Dwight Henderson

Lion in bed at night,
I can Bear-ly believe it!
I am a Giant of a man, a Chief.
Playing in the Super Bowl,
I soar like an Eagle,
Or maybe a Jet
And Ram through the line
To score the winning touchdown.
Voices from the sidelines:
"School comes first."
"You might get hurt."
"Nobody makes the NFL."
My parents don't understand
What football means to me.
They have no right to tackle my dreams.
I swear I'm gonna make it.
I'm gonna be a big star, All Pro.
But first I gotta make the high school team.

Dwight Henderson

When I first came to football camp,
I was thrown for a big loss.
I felt gang-tackled by
Three full workouts a day,
The bugs that blitzed me like linebackers,
The muscles that begged
To go on the injured-reserve list,
The coaches who yelled,
"Henderson, get the lead out."
"Henderson, you blew that play."
"Henderson, quit now and save us the trouble."
I had wanted to quit—every day,
But something inside of me
Wouldn't give them the satisfaction.
I took all the aches, all the abuse,
And when camp broke,
I had made the team.
I never had a better time in my life.

Dwight Henderson

"You look terrible," my mother said,
When I dragged my body home from practice.
"Why don't you quit?" she said.
"You never get to play anyway."
Good old Mom, right for the jugular.
I was too tired to answer.
"Look," she continued,
"Your grades would be higher.
You'd have some time for yourself and
God forbid, you could help some around the house."
"Leave me alone," I answered brilliantly.
Later, I started to think maybe she was right.
I'd have the time to hang out,
Like everybody else in high school.
And yet,
How do I explain to her that
Football is more than a game to me?
It's friends, excitement,
And the chance to be a high school hero.
Where else you gonna find that?

Dwight Henderson

The bench may be the best seat in the house.
But it's also the worst.
I spent a good part of the season there,
Afraid the coach would never send me in,
Afraid, also, that he would.
We had a good team in my senior year,
Even made the play-offs.
And in the final game,
When both running backs got hurt on the same play,
The coach called my number.
I ran to the huddle, nervous and thrilled.
The quarterback handed off to me.
I zipped left, then darted right,
Found daylight and scored the tying touchdown.
We lost that day 28–21.
Three years of practice for one play
May not sound like much,
But the slo-mo of that moment
Replays in loops
In the highlight film of my mind.
Showings every day.

Dwight Henderson

No Division I school knockin' at my door.
(Division 29 would be more like it.)
No big-time coach offerin' me a scholarship.
(More like scramblin' just to be a walk-on.)
Syracuse, Miami, Notre Dame:
Colleges of the mind,
Where other athletes zigzag toward glory
And the closest I can get to them
Will be watching them on TV on Saturday afternoons.
My dreams of big-time ball have fizzled out,
And I guess I'll have to be content
Bustin' through the line in some fraternity pickup game.
My mom says it's time to forget about football.
"Education is more important," she says.
She may be right, but I still feel crummy.
History quiz?
When? Today?
No, I didn't know about it.
Guess I'm past making history.

Yeah, I'm ditching Wiedermeyer's class.
What's he gonna do if I don't show up,
Shoot me?

Andrew Curran

When I told my father I had just won
Second prize in the freshman science fair,
He said, "That's nice, who won first prize?"
When I invited my mother to the exhibit,
She said, "Love to, dear, but I can't take off from work."
When I mentioned it to my grandfather,
He said, "Boy, oh, boy, but I don't see so good now."
Then he put on his best suit
And took my hand as I led him through
The maze of minivolcanoes and futuristic cars.
He announced to one and all,
"Have you seen my grandson's experiment?"
"Ssssh, Grandpa," I whispered loudly.
"What are you whispering about?" he said, even louder.
"People should see what you can do."
It's my grandfather with his bad eyes
Who can clearly see my future.
It's my grandfather who has made me feel
Like a prizewinner in life.

Andrew Curran

Hunched over my microscope in advanced biology,
I see a world under glass
Full of darting creatures.
No lab reports from them, I bet.
No tests,
No chores,
No worries.
With one touch I can make them
Bigger or smaller,
Clearer or imperceptible.
I can change their environment
At the drop of an eyedropper.
The power is mine.
Yet, suddenly,
I ask myself
Who's watching me under glass,
Adjusting the fine tuning?

Andrew Curran

People say that junior year is the toughest.
No lie, what with the SATs, AP courses, and
The pressure to start thinking about college.
I won first prize in the district science fair.
I studied the effects of electrolytes
On some species of tropical ferns.
I worked many long afternoons on it with
Mr. Gordon, the biology chairman.
"Look at it this way, Curran,
Consider it a trial run
For the Westinghouse competition next year," he said.
The only competition I wanted was a little
Three-man pickup game in the park with my friends.
I asked to leave early,
To trade my calculator for the courts
"Negative, Curran," Mr. Gordon said. "You're not
Sacrificing your talent for a few hoops."
I stayed, but you want to know something, Mr. G.?
I could be tempted to give up my high average
To hit the winning jump shot with one second left
In a varsity basketball game.

Andrew Curran

I want to be a NASA scientist
And ride the rocket
That slingshots me into space,
Hurtling toward a universe
Filled with mystery and majesty.
I pray the next world we inhabit
Will be better than the one we've spoiled.
I'd like to travel
Without weight, but with substance
To the far reaches of the galaxy.
I want to explore
What's out there waiting for me.
People make fun of me.
"You on the moon?
That figures, Curran,
You're already loony."
These people don't understand
The gravity of the situation.
They don't understand my dreams and thoughts,
So many dreams and thoughts that
Are out of this world.

Andrew Curran

(Thoughts on the way to history class.)

A last August memory
Of summer vacation:
Jetties stretching far out to sea,
Raindrops pitting the sand,
A longhaired girl in a black dress
Perches at the end of a line of rocks.
She ignores the waves
That pound against her pedestal,
Covering her with an umbrella spray of foam.
Call to her, dork,
Rescue her.
Sweep her off her unsteady precipice
And into your arms.
But before action, there are thoughts,
Too many thoughts.
And the minutes pass.
A lost moment that could have ended
The other empty moments of my life.

I'm just waiting
For the right moment
To grab the gun,
Just thinking and waiting.

98

_____ **Freshman**

Morton Potter

Chocolate,
Almond Joys, Snickers,
Potato Chips, Pizza, Cracker Jacks,
Onion Rings, Yodels, Ring Dings, Gummy Bears,
Eclairs, Sundaes, Necco Wafers, Ice Cream, Mounds,
Baby Ruths, Jelly Apples, Marshmallows, Milk Duds,
Milky Ways, French Fries, Cotton Candy,
M & M's, Licorice,
Vanilla

I'll start a diet,
Soon, I promise.
When?
Next Monday.
Or maybe,
The Monday after that,
Or maybe . . .
Never mind.
Food is too much
Fun.
I just can't help myself.

Morton Potter

I'm always late for first period,
Too heavy to sprint through the halls
And race up the stairs.
Gym is a particular torture for me.
The teacher doesn't say anything,
But I know what he's thinking:
He's praying I don't collapse
In the middle of exercise;
He'd have to fill out form after form.
My father went to this school.
Lean and trim, he lettered in three sports,
Said it was great,
With loads of parties, girls, and good times.
Maybe next year I'll find
The high school he's talking about.
"Perhaps if you lost some wei —" he
Starts to say, then stops,
Seeing the hurt look on my face.
I see the ashamed look on his.

Morton Potter

Being fat is a sin,
Original sin.
Here in class I sit on the chair,
Barely,
With parts of me hanging over the sides.
I am positive no one
Will ever get close to me,
Even if that were humanly possible.
It's not like I don't want to lose weight.
You name the diet and I've tried it.
But waves of blubber always return
To lap against my body.
I sit alone in the middle
Of an ocean of fat.
It is a sin what has happened to me,
What I've let happen.
I'm tired of pulling my weight
Around.

Morton Potter

In literature we learned
That an epiphany is a moment of truth
When the main character realizes in an instant
What his life is about.
It happened that my aunt
Said I should call up this girl,
The daughter of her bridge-club partner.
So I did and was rewarded
With a soft voice that
Laughed at my jokes and
Listened to my stories.
I felt thin talking to her.
But a few days later,
When I picked her up for a date
She suddenly developed a throbbing headache
And excused herself from my life forever.
It was clear that my aunt had neglected
To point out a few prominent physical details—
Mine.
I walked away from my near date in tears
And promised myself through the pain
That the next time my ship comes in
It will sail lightly
Atop the waves.

Morton Potter

I'm going to be late for history
Because in exercise class

```
                        b
                      e
                          n
        I'm              d
                      i
                    n
                  g
```

and s-t-r-e-t-c-h-i-n-g,
And p . . . . . ulling,
And sweat.

```
          .
        . ing,
```
All to find
A new,

```
          t
          h
          i
          n
```
                    Me!

Maybe I'll skip history
And run a few laps
Around the track.

Holly Lester

While other girls want to be
Cheerleaders or prom queens,
I want to play drums in a rock 'n' roll band.
While other girls dream of
College and the right clothes to wear,
I want to be on the road.
My father, a musician,
Left us when I was ten.
My mother, a social worker,
Figures my drumming is good therapy.
"It helps get out the anger," she says
With her usual psychobabble.
I tell her I'm not angry,
But seriously into my music.
Maybe one day I'll be playing with my own band
In a city I've never been to before,
And my father will walk in, sit next to me,
Then pick up his guitar and
Lead with a few riffs.
I'll follow his beat,
Playing out loud
The full measure of my love.

Holly Lester

My music teacher, Mr. Loomis,
Says everything in life has a beat—
The movement of the planets,
The change of the seasons,
Even the passing of kids in the hall.
Man, is he weird.
"You have to be sensitive to the music
Around you and the music within you," he says.
"You just have to let it flow out of you."
Man, is he crazy.
After we finished practicing
For the spring concert, he said,
"You are now in harmony
With the rest of the universe."
Man, is he off the wall.
Even though he is a sixties reject,
As he calls himself,
He is the best teacher I have.
He takes pieces of what I know,
Of what others know,
And fashions a seamless score
For everyone to enjoy.
Man, is he sharp.

Holly Lester

And now, live and in person,
Please give it up for
Holly Lester and the Jagged Edge Band.

> Poison in my heart,
> Poison in my heart,
> Poison in my heart,
> And it's all for you.
> You took my soul,
> My love, heaven-sent,
> You took my life,
> You took the rent.
> Poison in my heart,
> Poison in my heart,
> Poison in my heart,
> And it's all for you.

Sorry, Mr. Faber,
I was sort of daydreaming.
What was the question?
Why did Jay Gatsby throw those big parties?
I guess he liked the music?

Holly Lester

Never go out with a musician;
They're all losers.
All each one thinks about
Is his own instrument,
Or his own ego.
He may serenade you with sweet talk,
String you along,
And just when you think
You're in harmony with him,
The bum strikes a wrong chord
And pulls the plug
On your relationship.
No more romantic duets for me;
The last one broke my heart,
Playing around with my best friend.
You bet I'm singing solo from now on.
I'm not playing backup for any man again.
If I do meet someone new, someday,
I'm gonna make damn sure he's tone-deaf.
Never go out with musicians;
They're all losers.

Holly Lester

I could feel the passion
Rising slowly within me,
Like a small bubble growing,
Growing, then ready to burst
In a loud scream of ecstasy.
I could feel his eyes
Searching for me in the darkness,
His voice pleading, urging.
I could feel his hands
Stretching out for me.
I moved in time with him,
Our bodies pulsating to the same wild rhythms,
Sweat pouring down both of us.
That was the greatest night of my life.
I was *this* close to the lead singer;
I almost touched him,
And when he finished,
I collapsed in joy,
Spent.

What's all the racket about?
Can't you see I'm tryin' to sleep?
Wake me up later, I'm dead
Tired.

Denise Slattery

My boyfriend won't wear a condom.
He says it's like wearin' a catcher's mitt.
I says to him, "Either you get some
Or we ain't doin' it no more.
Don't you read the papers, pal?
There are all kinds of diseases,
And I don't want them in me, you hear?"
He says, "Don't you trust me?"
"Yeah, right," I says. "How do I know
All the ho's you slept with
Before you had the sense to hook up with me?"
He says, "I ain't got the money, babe."
I says, "They're free, jackass,
At the school, you just ask for 'em."
"Who, me? That's embarrassin'," he says.
"Get away from me, then," I says.
"All right, quit naggin', I'll get 'em."
"That's nice," I says, givin' him a quick kiss.
I swear, I ain't gonna take his crap, anymore,
Lyin' down.

Denise Slattery

I saw him with another girl—again.
    I'll knock his teeth out.
    I'll tear off his arm.
    I'll cut him off at the knees.
        Or someplace else.
    I'll scratch out his eyes.
    I'll punch him in the nose.
    I'll hit him in the stomach.
        Or someplace else.
    I'll club him on the shoulder.
    I'll pound him on the back.
    I'll kick him in the ass.
        Or someplace else.
Then,
And only then,
She can have
What's left of him.

Denise Slattery
Kevin Slattery

"How come you're home?"
    "Got suspended. A fight."
"Mom'll kill you, sis, you OK?"
    "Yeah, sure."
"Who'd you fight?"
    "Some stupid-assed girl, talkin' trash."
"You hurt her?"
    "Nah, just busted her up a bit."
"What you hit her with?"
    "A right. Like you showed me, Kevin.
    You serious about leavin'?"
"Told you last week. Got a friend out west
Who's gonna get me a job."
    "When you goin'?"
" 'Bout a week, that's what he says."
    "Spend it with me, Kev,
    I got lots of time now."
"Gotta go, kid, catch you later.
Maybe the two of us can have dinner, OK?"
    "OK."
            I don't want you to go, Kevin.
            Please don't go.

Denise Slattery

I don't need nobody,
You understand?
Nobody.
Just leave me alone.
You just stick to your teachin', Mr. Conroy,
And stay outta my personal business.
I don't care what you saw between
Me and my boyfriend.
Yeah, I'm back with him.
Just had a fight with him,
Nothin' unusual there.
I don't feel like movin' along to class.
What's the big deal if I'm late?
Late has a lotta different meanings.
What am I talkin' about?
You wouldn't understand.
Look, I don't need nobody
'Cept Joey right now.

112

Denise Slattery

I swear, little darlin',
You gonna have all the things I never had.
You gonna be all the things I never was.
Just because I screwed up my life
Don't mean I'm gonna screw up yours.
Got pregnant in my senior year.
What a graduation gift I got.
My mother wants to throw me outta the house, sayin'
"You can't live here no more. I done my share."
Just when all the doors 'round me seem to be closing,
My grammy opens up hers and says,
"Child, you bring your fat self down heah.
I'm gonna take care of you and the baby.
I miss little ones runnin' around this old house."
Nobody loves me
'Cept you, Grammy, and
You, my little darlin'.

What if I tell him
He can't be doin' this
Because of who's inside of me?

Douglas Atherton

They asked me to run for treasurer
Of the freshman class
Because nobody else wanted to run.
"Why are you doing it?" my friend Richie asked.
"I don't know," I said.
"Maybe I want to do something good."
"School government is such a joke, man," he said. "You're
Just a puppet for the school administration."
I won, unopposed,
And spent the year
Filling envelopes,
Writing newsletters,
Collecting dues.
I was impressed by my own importance.
Democracy would be a good thing, I think,
If it wasn't so boring.

114

Douglas Atherton

They asked me to run for secretary
Of the sophomore class
Because there were not many other candidates.
"You're still doing it?" my friend Richie asked. "Why?"
"I don't know," I said.
"I think I can make a difference."
"School government is such a joke, man," he said. "You're
Working so hard and nobody gives a damn."
I won against token resistance
And spent the year
Attending meetings,
Taking notes,
Writing minutes.
I was impressed by the democratic process.
School government is such a good thing, I think,
If you can convince more people to get involved.

Douglas Atherton

They asked me to run for vice-president
Of the junior class
Because other candidates had less experience.
"No, you're not doing it again?" my friend Richie asked.
"Why?"
"I don't know," I said.
"I think I can make positive changes."
"School government is such a joke, man," he said. "You're
Just fooling yourself. Get a life."
I won by a healthy margin
And spent the year
Cochairing council meetings,
Drafting speeches,
Attending district conferences.
I was impressed that the principal listened to us.
Changing people's opinions is a good thing, I think,
If you can get them to listen to you.

Douglas Atherton

They asked me to run for president
Of the senior class
Because I was the best candidate available.
"Don't tell me. Again?" my friend Richie asked. "Why?"
"I don't know," I said.
"I do know I'm the one who can get our fair rights."
"School government is such a joke, man," he said. "You're
Developing a Napoleonic complex, you know that?"
I won by a slim margin
And spent the year
Leading the student council,
Organizing the walkout,
Putting it to the principal.
I was impressed with how much I had accomplished.
Being president is a good thing, I think,
If most people would just listen to me.

Douglas Atherton

I couldn't get a date for the prom.
Too geeky, I guess.
But at the last moment
My friend Richie arranged a date for me,
A date that was drop-dead gorgeous, he said.
"Yeah, right," I said, until I saw her.
"You fixed me up with Alissa Hayley?
She's in my history class.
But definitely out of my league.
You sure she wants to go out with me?
Cool."
I did take her to the prom,
Even danced a couple of dances with her.
No matter she checked her watch over my shoulder
Before making polite excuses to run off with her friends.
Even so, for a few minutes at least,
She made me feel like a prince instead of a patsy.
It's something I'll remember with pride
As a highlight of my "brilliant" high school career.

Forget about brilliant high school career.
I'm not going to have any career at all.
I wish I had danced with her all night.

Teacher's Note #5
(My apologies to Stephen Crane)

Do not weep, colleague, for school is kind.
Because your students threw wild hands up in despair
And the frightened teacher ran home alone,
Do not weep.
School is kind.

    Hoarse booming sounds in the hall,
    Little souls who thirst for fight,
    These students were born to loiter and lie.
    Unexplained knowledge flies above them,
    Great is the incomprehension, great, in the school—
    A field where a thousand illiterates lie.

Do not weep, child, for school is kind.
Because your friends drop out,
Tumble in the streets, gulp, and die,
Do not weep.
School is kind.

    Slow-moving flags of futility,
    The Tower Tigers' banner of orange and black,
    These students were born to loiter and lie.
    Point to them the virtue of vacuity,
    Make plain to them the excellence of ignorance
    And a field where a thousand illiterates lie.

Mother, whose heart hangs heavily as a barrel
On the dull, spoiled reports of your failed son,
Do not weep.
School is kind.

Alissa Hayley

I hate Ms. Greely,
Ever since the first day of high school
When I walked into her English class
And she told me to drop my gum
In the wastepaper basket.
Then she said, "Young ladies are not cows,"
Which embarrassed me in front of everybody.
All term long she never cracked a smile,
Or told a joke,
Or let us get away with a single thing.
It was work, work, work every day.
All term long nothing but
Reading, book reports, and compositions,
And always my papers came back with
"This work is unacceptable. Please redo."
Boy, is she a witch.
I hope I never see her again.

Alissa Hayley

Oh, God, I got her again.
For sophomore English.
Why me?
One year of her wasn't enough?
Gimme a break!
I thought she would fail me last year,
But I managed to squeak out
A sixty-five on the final.
I made up all my missing homework
And even did an extra book report,
Which came back with the comment
"This is acceptable; you're improving."
I still hate her,
Maybe not so much.
We sort of put up with each other
And I think I caught her smiling once.
She's less of a witch,
But I hope I never see her again.

Alissa Hayley

Oh, no, this is too much.
You guessed it.
I got her again.
I am convinced that God has
A weird sense of humor.
I knew I would pass her class last year
I did all my homework on time
And even participated in a few class discussions.
We also had to do term papers
And I did mine on the Salem witch trials,
Which came back with the comment
"This is more than acceptable.
You've come a long way, Alissa."
I was very proud of that paper
Because I had worked so hard on it.
I don't think I hate her at all.
OK, she's not a witch.
Maybe I'll have her again next year.
I kinda hope so

Alissa Hayley

It figures.
Must be some kind of record.
Four years in a row—unbelievable.
She smiled when she saw me
On the first day of senior English.
"Good to see you, again, Alissa," she said.
The work didn't stop: more reading, more reports,
And a lot of preparation for the SATs.
I even wrote some pretty good poems
For my senior project, got a B+.
Near the end of the term,
She stopped me for a moment after class and said,
"Your work has been exceedingly acceptable.
In fact, I've nominated you
For an English department award at graduation."
I've come to realize that
Ms. Greely is the best teacher I ever had.
I'm sure gonna miss her next year.

Alissa Hayley

I couldn't choose a date for the prom.
Too picky, I guess.
But at the last moment
My friend Lisa arranged a date for me,
A date that was acceptable, she said.
"Yeah, right," I said, until I saw him.
"You fixed me up with Douglas Atherton?
He's in my history class.
But definitely minor league.
You sure I should go out with him?
All right."
I did let him take me to the prom,
Even danced a couple of dances with him.
No matter I checked my watch over his shoulder
Before making polite excuses to run off with my friends.
For a few minutes, at least,
I felt pathetic, not like a princess.
It's something I'll remember with shame
As a highlight of my "brilliant" high school career.

Forget about brilliant high school career.
I'm not going to have any career at all.
I wish I had danced with him all night.

Brad McCall

Varsity letter: Swimming

```
                        jump!
On the diving board I     a
                          n
                          d
              s-t-r-e-t-c-h o-u-t
                          a
                          n
                          d

                          w
                          i
                          t
                          h
                          o
                          u
                          t
      10
                          a

      perfect           i   p   e
                      r   p   l

          a
                          I

              sc   re
                 o
```

Brad McCall

Varsity letter: Tennis

Rallying	•	back
And	•	forth
Before	•	the
Big	•	match,
I	•	know
I	•	can
Take	•	their
Best	•	player,
6–0	•	6–0

Brad McCall

Varsity letter: Track

                              long
                    the   jump
              for   I
        off   fly
When I take   like a bird.

Brad **M**c**C**all

Varsity letter: Baseball

```
                    men
      Two                         on,


                    ___
           step                 up,
            I                   pow!
      ___                             ___
                  Home
                  ___
                  Run!
```

Brad McCall

Varsity Letter: Basketball

```
                                    l
                                 f  y
                                       and
                      left, let              d
I race downcourt,         to my              r
         cut            dribble              a
           to         crossover              i
          my      a                          n
         right, then
                                             i
                                             t
```

Man,
I don't want to go to
Wiedermeyer's class.
Think I'll go to the gym
And shoot a few hoops.

129

Freshman

Renata Reznitskaya

(In translation)

Where I came from
There is no country.
Where I've been
You could not comprehend.
Cold nights,
Long lines,
Hope buried under permafrost and
Trampled by bureaucrats
Who would not let me study in school
Or let my father advance in his career.
My family, having little but patience,
Managed, finally, to get papers
To come to this sunlit country.
I have shivered through
The long night of my childhood.
I am now ready, like a winter rose,
To bloom in the warm earth
Of my new country.

Renata Reznitskaya

I am, how you say,
Pulled in opposite directors.
Oh, directions, thank you.
Over one hand,
Excuse me, on one hand,
My mother takes me
To visit revelations
Oh, relatives, thank you,
Who have come here before us,
Who drink tea through cubes of sugar.
On the other hand,
I want to be totally American,
Visit with my new friends
Who dance in hottest clubs
And have lots of money.
I tell my father
This, for sure, is a great country.
"For you, my daughter, not for me," he says,
Sitting in his chair, not visiting anyone.

Renata Reznitskaya

"You are happy here?" my father asks.
"Yes, very much, Papa."
"You like the school?"
"Yes, very much.
I am doing well in all my subjects."
"Yes, I know, I see your reports."
Something bad is coming.
I look at his eyes and feel a chill wind.
He sits down across from me,
Takes my hand and a deep breath and says,
"I must go back."
"To what?" I cry. "There is nothing there."
"There is nothing here."
"For how long?"
"I do not know; I will write."
His letters come frequently,
But paper words do not fill
Hole in my heart.
Will he ever come back?
Will he see me graduate?
I read his letters over and over again.

132

Renata Reznitskaya

My mother promises me over tea
One day men will look in my eyes
And find the beauty living there.
American men do not, I fear,
Have developed sense of romantic geography.
They look at everything but my eyes—
My breasts, lips, legs, and hair—
As if I come in parts
Ready to be assembled for their satisfaction.
Do I think Russian men are better?
Maybe a little.
But they just use a different language
To make the same mistakes.
Mama,
How will I find someone who loves me,
Someone who will not make for me false promises,
Lying in wait for the time
He can have all parts
Together in the dark?
All parts,
Except the beauty in my eyes.

Renata Reznitskaya

I am to graduate
And in September
I go to a college
That is not too far away.
I am to study pharmacy
And maybe one day I work
In hospital or laboratory.
But more important than college
Is news that Papa came back to us.
"There is nothing for me there, either," he says.
"Also to miss your graduation
Would be a terrible crime, no?"
"It is not so great a thing," I say, blushing.
"It *is* the greatest thing," he corrects.
My papa and I sit together in the kitchen,
Drinking tea through cubes of sugar.
I am so happy,
My life, flowers of same family
Rooted together and climbing heavenward
To meet the sky-blue future.

I will never see Papa again.

Teacher's Note #6

Let me see,
What to pack in my book bag for my classes today.
An apple for the teacher?
I don't think so.
Pencils, pens, notebooks?
Never carry 'em.
Ruler, compass, protractor?
Only for nerds.
I only pack what is essential:
One box cutter (weapon of choice),
One switchblade (get the point?),
One ice pick (cool, cool),
One can of Mace (for your face),
One can of spray paint (you need refinishing),
One cherry bomb (a real blast),
One razor blade (look sharp),
And, of course, my trusty .25.
It's a tight fit,
But I can throw out my texts.
I don't need them for
Survival.

Justin Singleberry

If the light is right,
I can catch my mother's face
On my sketch pad as she tells me,
"There's no future in art."
If the light is right,
I can catch my father's face
On my sketch pad as he tells me,
"There's no future in art."
I like my first year of high school,
Though I wish I had some art classes.
But I sometimes have the feeling
I don't fit within the lines of
The paint-by-numbers routine.
I'd like to spend my whole life drawing
With a free hand.

Justin Singleberry

I'd like to be a medieval monk
With a medieval manuscript.
I'd sit, looking at the precious page
With a capital *I* on it.
Illuminated, the *I* would be
Brocaded by seraphim and flowers,
Curlicues and puffy clouds.
Mental gymnastics by the hour.
I feel the room is cold; my hand is pale;
I stare transfixed at my line.
Frightened, I sense the specter of death
Running headlong down my spine.

Justin Singleberry

This year I've joined the school paper
As the cartoonist-in-residence.
I found there is a fine line
Between right and wrong
And I draw it.
Things are never black and white,
But shades of gray
And I draw them.
School politicians never say what they mean,
But I do,
In neatly printed letters and balloons.
In broad strokes I capture all their excesses,
Deflating their pompous speeches
With my acid-tipped pen.
I never run out of material.
It's all there on the front page,
Ready to be satirized.
With my cartoons, I love to get
To the art of the matter.

138

Senior

Justin Singleberry

I really didn't want to go to the prom at all,
But my mother ordered me to go,
For appearance' sake, she said.
When she caught Evan and me together,
She beat me silly.
"What did I do to deserve this?" she screamed.
I couldn't give her an answer.
Besides, that's not the important question.
For appearance' sake
I'll go to the prom with Gloria.
She and I are good friends.
Maybe Evan will be there.

Justin Singleberry

Death may come in Venice,
Or in the afternoon,
Or for the salesman.
It will come for me
From my friend Evan.
Nobody knows,
Not even my parents,
Who worry about my college tuition next year.
It's a needless worry.
I'd like to go to Paris and paint
Before the color of life fades,
Before the canvas wrinkles and cracks.
I'd like to draw strength from the old masters
And tell them I'll soon be able
To picture them in person.

Mr. Wiedermeyer,
Let us out of here, please.
I have an appointment in Paris.

Franklin Waters

My moms once read me a poem
About this lady whose life
"Ain't been no crystal stair."
"What's a crystal stair?" I ask.
"The way to a better life. Why you
Think I be workin' so hard—
So you can play video games all day long?
Go to the library."
"Mama, it's Sunday, library's closed."
"Don't be such a wiseass," she says. "I have
A dream—"
"Ma, I know that one."
"—for you. Don't be interruptin' me. You just
Started high school and I want you
To climb all the stairs you can."
"They got elevators, Ma."
I love my mama.
Someday I gonna get her a place of her own
Where she can read and recite all the poetry she wants
In every room of the house.

Franklin Waters

I live with my mother
And my two brothers in the projects.
Every day I can hear
The wail of police sirens,
The splatter of automatics,
The arguments of drug dealers,
All happenin' in my 'hood.
You, white boy, drive to school.
You don't know nothin'
'Bout dodgin' bullets,
Steppin' on vials,
Lookin' out for the police.
My mother don't allow my little brothers
To play on the streets, day or night.
She hardly lets me out.
What she gonna do?
Keep me locked up forever?
But, white boy,
You and me gonna get to school at the same time.
I'm gonna cross the street to my education
Without gettin' caught in the cross fire.

Franklin Waters

School's OK, but kind of borin'.
You sit in one class after another
And some of the teachers
Don't know you're alive.
Some days I skip school and hang out.
I got this one friend, Anton, from the block,
Who says to me, "What you goin' to school for?
It ain't gonna get you no job."
I tell him it ain't that bad.
I kinda like science and gym.
He says, "You playin' yourself.
What them teachers gonna give you?"
"A diploma," I answer.
"That and a token gets you on the bus," he sneers.
I walk with him to the courts
And we spend the afternoon playin' one-on-one.
I think shootin' threes is more fun than school.
So I miss a few classes.
It don't matter much.

Franklin Waters

It's all messed up,
In school and outta school,
All over the place.
My moms found out
I was cutting class
And she broke on me.
My friend Anton got shot
And then got hisself arrested
For breaking and entering.
And in science, my favorite class,
My teacher, Ms. Crosser,
Accused me of cheatin'
Just because I got ninety-six on her test.
"You couldn't have gotten
This grade by yourself," she said.
"Why, because I'm black?" I shot back.
"I didn't mean it that way," she stammered.
Like hell she didn't.
I feel all messed up.
It ain't worth it; I'm outta here;
I quit.

Franklin Waters

"Hey, pal, do I look like the waitress?"
    Two eggs over easy, takes French.
"Ellen, paying customer at the counter."
    Chicken salad on rye, no mayo.
"Cheeseburger, burn it, I got it."
    Adam and Eve on whole wheat.
"Yeah, you look familiar, too, history class, right?"
    Cowboy, with a draw up front.
"Me? Ain't been there in weeks, got this job."
    Stretch one.
"You graduatin' next week? That's cool."
    Meatloaf platter, extra gravy.
"Job ain't bad, gets crazy sometimes."
    Grilled cheese with ham, to go.
"See you around."

"Ellen, pick up,
They ain't gonna pay for no cold food."
Wish I was back in history class right now.
Lookin' at Wiedermeyer got to be better than
Lookin' at this grill.

Teacher's Note #7

I speak.
Who listens?
I teach.
Who cares?
A child of my loins,
A child of my class.
One untouched by personal teaching,
One untouched by public teaching.
>Who wrote *The Diary of Anne Frank*?
>Did Alexander the Great invent the telephone?
>Why was the Boer War so dull?
>Is the Peace Corpse still alive?
>Why didn't the colonists drink coffee instead?
>Did people wear coats during the Cold War?
>Where *is* the Leaning Tower of Pizza?
Those who forget the past
Are condemned to repeat it,
Term after term after term.
There is little I can do to turn the tide.
There is little I have done to make a difference.

Devonne Elliot

My name has a shadow attached to it.
Four years before I was born
My parents buried a baby boy
Who died when he was fifteen months old.
His name was Devon.
They speak of him sometimes:
How he walked before he was a year old,
How he had just started to talk,
How his smile made you smile in return.
Amid tears, they bring out his photo album
On his birthday and in the afternoon
Place flowers on his small grave.
My parents treat me like a fragile package.
I bring home excellent grades.
My parents are pleased,
But I know the unstated question:
What great triumphs
Would Devon have brought home?

Devonne Elliot

There are people in my class
Who would sell their grandmothers downriver
For two points higher on an exam.
There are people in my class
Who write notes on their palms
For four points higher on an exam.
There are very few honors classes at Tower,
But in those advanced classes
The competition is cutthroat.
I'm not learning for the sake of knowledge,
But for the sake of getting into a good college.
Welcome to the vulture class.
We have a talon for
Tearing each other apart.
I guess I will just have to
Carrion.

Devonne Elliot

It's not too early to think about college.
It's not too early to check out
Which college I want.
I have to deal with a whole bunch of new initials —
GPA, FAF, SAT.
I worry about my college essay.
Will I be able to strike the right chord
Between truthful bragging and sincere humility?
Will I dazzle them with my
Verbal virtuosity,
Great determination,
Perceptive vision,
Matchless grace?
Who am I kidding
As my wastepaper basket
Fills with crumpled drafts?
It all comes down to one single question:
Will they like me?

Devonne Elliot

(Excerpts from Salutatory Speech—Draft I)

Welcome parents, friends, and teachers,
To our graduation celebration.
We are celebrating four years of hard work,
Four years of friendships,
Four years of fun and memories.
We, the graduates, are living proof that
The teenagers of today
Are the responsible adults of tomorrow.
Let me share with you some . . .

(Thoughts I'll have while presenting my speech next week)

So nervous . . .
I hope I don't screw this up. . . .
The lights are so hot. . . .
Where are my parents sitting. . . ?
Can't wait 'til this is over. . . .
Missed valedictorian by four hundredths of a point. . . .
Slow down, you're rushing it . . .
Party all night . . .
Just going to chill all summer . . .
Come on, Devon, you and I are going to college.

150

Devonne Elliot

Come on, Devon.
You'll be with me in spirit
As I go off to college in the fall.
I can't wait for the summer to fly by
So I can meet my roommates,
Buy my books in the campus store,
Take long walks by the river,
And watch the racing shells
Skim the water like dragonflies.
All my late nights,
All my hard work,
All my studying—
It was worth it!
I am going to an Ivy League school.
Me, me, little old me.
I feel like hugging myself all summer.

Oh no, oh no.
Please, Mr. Wiedermeyer,
Don't mess things up for me.
It's not fair, not fair at all.

Eddie Kellerman

At my Bar Mitzvah last year,
Just after the rabbi spoke,
My father read a poem he had written.
I know my father's words by heart:
    Eddie has grown up before my eyes.
    His words, which used to fall like building blocks,
    Are now resonant and strong.
    My mind whirs and sees pictures of
    You streaking across a soccer field;
    You, age six, signing your first library card;
    You giving a speech to the whole fourth grade assembly;
    You learning to swim.
    All these pictures I recall
    As you stand before family and friends
    Reciting so beautifully the ancient words.
    Go with my love and blessing.
    A child has given us touching memories.
    A man shall now focus on his own life;
    He shall now make his own pictures.
    Eddie has grown up before my eyes.
My father's words have lasted a lot longer than
The fountain pen the rabbi gave me.

Eddie Kellerman

I've been grounded for two weeks.
I can't go to my friends' houses.
I can't hang out after school.
It's not fair.
My friend Jeremy
Had this party last Saturday
And I kind of lost track of time.
Besides, my eyes were not on the clock,
But on the face and body of Lori,
A new friend of Jeremy's.
I think I'm in love.
When I got home at 5 A.M.,
My parents pounced on me.
"What were you thinking of?" they said together.
"Lori," I said to myself.
I've been grounded for two weeks.
It was worth it.

Eddie Kellerman

My parents hassle me about everything.
Now it's the SAT,
Which, I try to tell them,
I don't take 'til next year anyway.
They want me to memorize a thousand words.
They want me to take a review course.
They want me to be some brainiac I'm not.
What does the SAT really mean?
>Stupidity And Tension?
>Scars And Traumas?
>Sorrow And Tears?
Will I have to walk around forever
With my mark branded on my forehead?
Will my sure-to-be mediocre score
Trail after me like a bad credit rating?
I can't stand it!
SAT.
I fear and *loathe* you.
(See, I don't need a test
To reach the *pinnacle* of my *potential*.)
Ma, please leave me alone.
There's no way I'm getting into Harvard.

Eddie Kellerman

"Where are you going?" my mother asked.
"Out," I said.
"Where, out? You never tell me anything."
My mother knows I shoot pool sometimes,
But she doesn't want to hear about it.
So I don't tell her.
Jeremy was driving me home afterwards.
We didn't see the other car.
It spun us around, once, twice,
Like an amusement park ride.
Glass cracked into little mosaic tiles.
When the ambulance came,
The paramedics checked us over.
One of them said, "You boys were lucky,
Just scratches, but we're taking you in anyway."
From the hospital emergency room,
Still feeling shaken up,
I dialed home and said,
"Mom, I got something to tell you. . . ."

Eddie Kellerman

Can't believe I'm graduating in a few days.
The year went by so fast.
What's next? Wiedermeyer?
I can handle it.
I'm still recovering from the prom last weekend.
Man, what a blast:
My parents taking pictures like crazy;
The limo driver calling me sir.
And Lori, the most beautiful girl in the world,
Telling me how handsome I looked in my tux.
My friend Jeremy said
The prom was a waste of money.
I told him it was the most wonderful night of my life.
Before long, I'll have to be an adult,
Go to college (not Harvard),
Get a good job.
But right now I don't want to think of all that.
I just want to think of the good time
I had at the prom
When the music and dance of life
Went on and on all night.
And Lori kissed me like there was no tomorrow.

My God, he's gonna kill us.
He's gonna kill us all.

THE CLASH

June **16**th

12:00 P.M.

Bruno Willis, spectator

Man, this is borin'.
I've been standin' here for two freakin' hours
And nothin', man.
Just a whole lot of hangin' around.
Cops and doctors and stuff sittin' on their asses.
I seen a guy I seen on TV,
Some news guy, know what I'm sayin'?
Didn't give me no autograph or nothin'.
Screw him.
What do I want?
I want to see some action, man.
You know,
Someone gettin' shot,
Someone jumpin' from a window,
Someone screamin' bloody murder.
You know,
Action, man,
Just like it is in the movies,
Know what I'm sayin'?

Vinnie Delvecchio, parent

He's still in there?
What does he have to complain about?
Do I get the summers off?
Do I get out at three?
Do I get all the holidays?
Do I always get the day shift?
Yeah, tell me about it,
As I cash my unemployment check.
Tell me, what does he have to complain about?
What other job has such benefits?
What other job is so clean?
What other job is for life?
What other job is so respected?
Yeah, don't tell me about it.
I don't wanna hear it.
Would I be a teacher?
Not on your life.
Who wants to teach these kids all day?
They're animals.

Harry Balinger, police captain
Frank Picardi, emergency unit

What do we know?
>More than last time.

You place the mike?
>Yeah, through an air duct.

What did you pick up?
>Mostly soft crying. No panic.

Any indication of multiple weapons?
>We think there's only one gun involved.

What's he doing with it?
>He seems to be just picking it up,
>Putting it down. Real strange.

Threatening anyone?
>Not overtly, but he's not letting them go either.

We're trying to contact his family.
>He mentioned a Michael last time, who's that?

Someone in his class? I'm not sure.
>Do we go in?

No, not now, just sit tight.
>What was that? Sounded like a gunshot.

Hold your fire, I repeat, hold your fire.
>Captain, should we bust down the door?

No, wait, sit tight. Wait, wait, it's quiet again.
Find out where that shot came from.
If we rush in now, he might kill everyone.

Teacher's Note #8

An accident, repeat, an accident.
Nobody's hurt, I swear it.
You see, I'm not too familiar with guns,
Not like Michael —
He knows everything.
I was just practicing loading and unloading
When it went off.
There's a bullet hole in the ceiling now.
Trust me, I'll pay for the damage.
Let me assure you,
All the students are fine.
No one got hurt,
But they were a bit shaken by the noise.
And I do believe some of the students are thirsty.
If it is not too much trouble,
Do you think you could send in a student
With some water?
I would be most grateful.
I was just loading and unloading the gun
When it went off.
I was deciding whether the bullet was for me
Or someone else.
I really need a few more minutes to make up my mind.
Trust me, I'll pay for the damage.

Harry Balinger, police captain

That's it, that's our in,
I want a
> Nike-wearing,
> Walkman-hearing,
> Slang-talking,
> Brave-stalking,
>> Baby-faced cop.

I want a
> Cool hand,
> Red headbanded,
> Baggy-wear,
> Friendly stare,
>> Baby-faced cop.

I want a
> Clean shaven,
> No misbehavin',
> Quick actin',
> Pistol-packin',
>> Baby-faced cop
Who can recognize both
> The goodness of a man's heart and
> The darkness of his soul,
And quickly decide
Whether to talk to the guy
Or take him out.
We got anybody like that?

David Rush, TV reporter
Harry Balinger, police captain

CHANNEL 5 HAS JUST LEARNED A SHOT OR SHOTS HAVE BEEN FIRED IN THE CLASSROOM WHERE A VETERAN TEACHER IS HOLDING HIS HISTORY CLASS HOSTAGE. WE DON'T KNOW IF THERE ARE ANY CASUALTIES. WE DON'T KNOW IF THERE ARE ANY DEATHS. I SEE CAPTAIN BALINGER, THE RANKING OFFICER ON THE SCENE. MAYBE HE'LL SPEAK TO US.

Q: CAPTAIN BALINGER, WHAT CAN YOU TELL US?

A: NOT MUCH. WE KNOW ONLY ONE SHOT HAS BEEN FIRED. WE KNOW THERE ARE NO CASUALTIES. WE KNOW THAT THE BULLET CAME FROM INSIDE THE ROOM.

Q: EXCUSE ME, BUT HOW DO YOU KNOW ALL THAT?

A: I AM NOT AT LIBERTY TO SAY.

Q: ARE YOU NOW GOING TO STORM THE
CLASSROOM?

A: I'D RATHER NOT SPECULATE ON OUR
OPT—

Q: EXCUSE ME, CAPTAIN, I'M GETTING WORD TO
THROW IT BACK TO THE STUDIO, WHERE, I
UNDERSTAND, FIREMEN ARE BATTLING A
TERRIFIC BLAZE IN MIDTOWN. WE'LL GET BACK
TO YOU—I PROMISE.

Teacher's Note #9

Years ago,
When I walked into my first class,
All the students rose and said,
"Good morning, sir."
I turned around to see
Who else had come into the room.
Then,
I had youth, energy, and patience.
I had something to say.
I had something to teach.
Now,
My lessons are reruns.
My patience is gone.
And my thoughts scare me.
I do not know what is left to teach.
I do not know what I can give my students.
I feel myself skittering on
The knife-edge of despair.

James Sánchez, police officer

He was at his desk when I entered,
Lecturing frozen-in-headlights students
On some provisions of the Constitution.
"Michael, can you answer that?" he asked.
No Michael, they all knew—
As eyes darted from him to me,
I placed the water on his desk.
I saw the gun in his hand,
Pointed first at the class, then at his head.
I felt the gun in my book bag.
"What is your name?" he asked, not unkindly.
A crazy thought—"Michael," I said.
"Michael?" he said, surprised.
"How wonderful you look.
Come here, my boy."
He pointed his gun at me.
I thought any second now he would fire.
"Got a present for you, Pop,
Here in my bag," I said, gently.
I quickly pulled out my service revolver
And shot him in the shoulder.
"Michael?" he said again, "Why?"
As he fell wounded across the desk,
Knocking over the water,
The water he had wanted for his class.

Harry Balinger, police captain

I want this room secure,
And I want an ambulance now!
Do you hear me?
No one enters until I know
The extent of injuries,
The limits of lunacy.
Before they are mauled by parents and press,
I want to know
What each student has to say.
I want to understand
What happened here.
Was there a reason for this madness?
And make damn sure of this:
I want Mr. Wiedermeyer's wound taken care of,
Quickly and professionally.
Then arrest him and read him his rights.
I'll talk to him later, in the ER.
Anyone who screws this up will have me in his face.
Got that?

Patti Bennett

He was gonna kill us.
I swear he was gonna kill us.
He was acting crazy,
Like he was talking to us,
And not talking to us.
I want my papa.
Where is he?

Derek Bain

Hey, man, no sweat.
I knew we were cool.
You see the dude who shot Mr. W.?
Right in the shoulder.
Is the guy a cop or something?
Is this gonna be on TV?

Rhonda Ellis

Did you see that?
Just like in the movies.
Hey, you think they'll make
A movie outta this?
My hands are so cold.

Omar Clarkson

Officer,
What do I do now?
Where do I go?
Please tell me what to do.

Esther Torres

Dear, sweet Jesus,
I thought you were about to call me.
I was ready, you know.
But you said, Not yet, my child.
I will wait patiently for you.

Kathleen Gennaro

That bastard,
Who the hell does he think he is?
What did he do that for?
Scarin' us like that.
I'm glad he got shot.
He should die.

Cory Deshayes

Kathleen, don't leave me,
Don't go.
I don't wanna be alone,
Now.

Wing Li Wu

Even if I knew English better,
I would not have the words.
I do not have the words.
Did they have to shoot the teacher?
He was such a nice man.

Andrew Curran

Why didn't I do anything?
I was so close to the man.
I could've knocked the gun away.
I did nothing—
Once again.
Yeah, I know, nobody did anything.
That doesn't help me.

Holly Lester

Let me outta here.
Man, am I gonna party tonight.
Don't even ask me what I'm gonna do.
I'll be in no condition to tell you.
All I know is,
The music's never gonna stop.

Denise Slattery

Kevin,
Kevin,
Where'd you go?
You gotta come for me
And take me to Grammy's house, now.

Douglas Atherton

What would I like?
If it's not too much trouble,
A drink of water, please.
What happened?
I don't remember what happened,
None of it.

Alissa Hayley

I'd like to go home, please.
Is it cold in here?
I can't stop shaking.
Can you get Ms. Greely
And tell her to call my mother?
Please.

Renata Reznitskaya

I do not understand.
Why did he do this to us?
Did we make him angry in some way?
He acted like a lunatic,
Pointing a pistol
And repeating this name, Mikhail,
Michael, I think you say in English.

Justin Singleberry

I don't want to go to Paris.
I don't want to go anywhere.
Just let me go to my room.
I don't want to see anyone,
Except Evan.

Devonne Elliot

Shows you, man.
You can't trust anyone these days,
Except yourself.
That was close, too close.
I just want to sleep
And pretend this was a bad dream.

Eddie Kellerman

What are those lights for?
Get 'em away from me.
It was no big deal in there,
Absolutely nothin' goin' on.
The guy kept us.
He got shot.
End of story.
No, man, I don't know who Michael is.
I don't much freakin' care.

Sherwood Cowley, principal

Mr. Wiedermeyer's been shot?
You've got to be kidding me.
What can I tell the press?
How can I preserve the good name of my school?
Look, we're no better or worse
Than other city schools.
We've kept the number of
Fights and muggings
Down to a respectable level.
We've improved our math and reading scores.
We've installed metal detectors at the front door.
We've beefed up our internal security.
Look, every school has its problems—
We're no different.
Mr. Wiedermeyer's been shot?
I'll tell the press that.
People will be relieved.
How dare he tarnish the good name of my school?

David Rush, TV reporter

THIS JUST IN! THE HOSTAGE CRISIS AT TOWER
HIGH SCHOOL IS OVER. WE HAVE LEARNED THAT
ALL THE CHILDREN HAVE EMERGED FROM THEIR
BRUTAL ORDEAL SAFE AND SOUND. ONE MIGHT
SUSPECT THAT A MEDIA BIDDING WAR FOR THEIR
EXCLUSIVE STORIES WILL SOON BEGIN. ONE
CAN ONLY IMAGINE THE SUFFERING THESE
CHILDREN HAVE ENDURED AT THE HANDS OF
THIS DERANGED PSYCHOPATH. AS FOR THE
GUNMAN HIMSELF, LITTLE IS KNOWN. WE HAVE
HAD REPORTS HE HELD A GRUDGE AGAINST
THE BOARD OF EDUCATION, DEMANDED TWO
MILLION DOLLARS IN TENS AND TWENTIES,
WANTED TO FREE FOREIGN NATIONALS HELD
IN U.S. PRISONS. BUT LET US RETURN TO THE
IMPORTANT STORY, THE SAFE RETURN OF THESE

YOUNGSTERS. I THINK I NOW SEE ONE POOR
VICTIM IN THE ARMS OF HER PARENTS. LET'S
THANK GOD THIS STORY HAS A HAPPY ENDING.

Cosmo Gennaro, parent

I'm glad the bastard's been shot.
He got what he deserved.
How did they let that man
Become a teacher in the first place?
Don't they screen out wackos?
I tell you, when I was a kid,
We respected our teachers—
We didn't talk back to them.
And if we did,
We caught hell from our parents.
Nowadays, school don't mean nothin',
Not to students, not to teachers.
It's just somethin' to go through.
Nobody cares what happens in there,
As long as the kids are off the streets.
My own daughter who got locked up with that maniac
Ain't learnin' nothin' she can use.
How's the school gonna get any better
If they ain't teachin'?
And they let wackos in besides?
I'm glad the bastard's been shot.
He got what he deserved.

Frank Picardi, emergency unit

Captain Balinger?
You look beat.
Want a cup of coffee?
The principal can speak to the press for now.
Nothing but a circus out there—
Reporters fighting over kids,
Who are hugging their parents,
Who are pushing away the reporters.
I want to show you what we just found
In Wiedermeyer's locker:
A poem and a newspaper clipping
From a paper out west,
Dated about a year ago.
You look at 'em, sir.
And take a few minutes.
You know, there's nothing more
You could've done.

For Michael

Somewhere before the end,
Somewhere between childhood and adulthood,
I lost you.
Somewhere between your first step and last step,
I walked right past.
Somewhere between your first word and last word,
I did not hear you.
For other children I taught my subject,
For other children I tried to show
History did not start at the moment of their births.
Some listened,
Most didn't.
What did I teach them, give them?
What did I teach you, give you?
Oh, Michael,
I should have taught you better.
I should have taught you how to save yourself.
I gave you everything I had.
It wasn't nearly enough.

Local Man Drowns In Killer Surf

Police divers today recovered the body of a local man, Michael Wiedermeyer, 27, who several hours earlier had braved the rough water, ignoring repeated attempts by people onshore to call him back.

"He must have been crazy to go out that far," said one eyewitness who did not give his name.

"That, or he must have been trying to kill himself," another eyewitness added.

An autopsy will be performed, police officials indicated. They refused to speculate on whether this was a suicide or a tragic accident.

The victim, Michael Wiedermeyer, was relatively new to the area and "was looking for employment, though he spent a lot of time walking up and down the beach," according to one source.

Mr. Wiedermeyer's parents have been notified and are en route to claim their son's body.

"I don't care how old a child is," one bystander remarked sadly. "No parent should outlive his child. You never recover from that."

Harry Balinger, police captain

You read the headlines in the newspaper,
The headlines that will be forgotten by tomorrow:
>"Teacher Goes Berserk;
>Hold Class Hostage;
>Shot Down By Police;
>Children Safe, but Shaken"

Private tortures
Ending in public spectacle.
Serpentine demons
Strangling common sense.
Mr. Wiedermeyer,
I now realize the *whys*,
Somewhat.
I now realize the pain you went through,
To a degree.
Yet, if I were one of the students,
I'd never forgive.
If I were the judge, I'd never let you out.
But, if I were your friend,
I'd say to you in your cell,
Read your books, and think of the good days
When you were younger and Michael was alive
And the world was bright with promise.
"Go in soft peace, Mr. Wiedermeyer,
Go in soft peace.
We are all safe now."